a minedition book
published by Penguin Young Readers Group

Published simultaneously in Canada.
Manufactured in Hong Kong by Wide World Ltd.
Designed by Michael Neugebauer
Typesetting in Veljovic, designed by Jovica Veljovic.
Color separation in Japan.

Library of Congress Cataloging-in-Publication Data available upon request.

ISBN 0-698-40010-0
10 9 8 7 6 5 4 3

For more information please visit our website: www.minedition.com

The Ugly Duckling

Hans Christian Andersen
with Pictures by Robert Ingpen
Translated from the Danish by
Anthea Bell

Jubilee Edition
200 years Hans Christian Andersen

It was lovely out in the country. Summer had come; the wheat in the fields was golden, the oats were still green, and the new-mown hay had been built into haystacks in the meadow, where the storks walked around on their long red legs talking to each other in Egyptian. Egyptian was the language they had learned from their mothers. The fields and meadows were surrounded by a great forest, with deep lakes among the trees. Yes, it was really beautiful out in the country!

An old castle with a deep moat lay in the sunshine. Large dock plants grew between the castle walls and the water. They were so tall that small children could stand upright under the biggest of them. It was like being in a dense and trackless forest among those dock leaves, and there a duck sat on her nest. She was supposed to be hatching out her little ducklings, but she was getting rather bored. Hatching the eggs took so long, and she didn't have many visitors. The other ducks thought it was more fun to swim in the moat than go to see her and sit under a dock leaf talking.

At last one of the eggs cracked, and then another and another. "Cheep, cheep!" All the egg yolks had turned into live little ducklings putting their heads out of the shells.

"Quack, quack!" said the mother duck, and they immediately began looking all around them under the green leaves. Their mother let them stare their fill, because green is good for the eyes.

"Oh, what a big world this is!" said all the young ducklings, for they had much more room now than when they were still inside their eggs.

"You don't think this is the whole world, do you?" said their mother. "Dear me, no, the world goes all the way to the other side of the garden and the pastor's field, although I've never been as far as that myself. Now, have you all arrived?" And she raised herself a little way off her nest. "Oh no, I see you haven't. The biggest egg is still there. How much longer is it going to take, I wonder? I'm getting really tired of this!" And she settled back on the nest again.

"Well, how are you doing?" asked an old duck who had dropped in for a visit.

"This last egg is taking so long!" said the duck on her nest. "It just won't crack. But do look at the others! The sweetest little ducklings I ever saw, the very image of that rascal their father who never comes to see me."

"Let me have a look at the egg that won't hatch," said the old duck. "Ah, that's a turkey egg, you take my word for it! I fell for the same trick once, and oh, the trouble I had with those turkey chicks! Turkeys are afraid of the water, you see! I just couldn't get them to go in. I quacked and I pecked, but it was no use. Now, let's have another look at your egg. Oh yes, a turkey egg and no mistake. You leave it where it is and teach your other children to swim!"

"Oh, I'll sit on it a little longer," said the duck. "I've been sitting on this nest so long already, I might as well stay here until they bring in the hay harvest!"

"As you like," said the old duck, and she went away.

At last the big egg cracked. "Cheep, cheep!" said the duckling as he tumbled out. He was very big and very ugly. The mother duck looked at him. "What a dreadfully big duckling!" she said. "The others don't look like that! Maybe he's a turkey chick after all! Oh well, we'll soon find out. He's going into the water even if I have to kick him in myself."

Next day the weather was very fine; the sun shone on the green dock leaves, and the mother duck went down to the moat with her whole family. Splash! She jumped into the water. "Quack, quack!" she said, and duckling after duckling flopped into the water after her. It washed over their heads, but they came straight up again and were soon swimming very well. Their legs paddled away as if they knew just what to do, and now they were all out on the water. Even the ugly grey duckling was swimming.

"No, he's not a turkey," said the mother duck. "See how well he paddles his legs and how upright he holds himself? He's my own duckling, and he's really very handsome if you look at him properly. Quack, quack! Now, come along with me, all of you, and I'll take you out into the world and introduce you to the poultry yard. But keep close to me in case anyone treads on you, and mind you watch out for the cat!"

So they went into the poultry yard. It was very noisy there because two duck families were fighting over an eel-head, but in the end the cat carried it off.

"That's the way of the world!" said the mother duck, licking her bill because she would have liked to eat the eel-head herself. "Now, come along and hurry up," she said. "You must bow to the old duck over there. She is the grandest bird in the poultry yard. She's of Spanish blood, which is why she is so fat, and as you can see she has a red rag around her leg. That is the greatest mark of distinction any duck can be given, and it means she won't be killed and eaten. Animals and human beings alike know what a superior duck she is! Come along, quack! And don't turn your feet in – well-brought-up ducklings waddle with their legs wide apart, just like their parents. Now, bend your necks and quack!"

And so they did, but the other ducks in the yard looked at them and said in loud voices, "Well, look at this! I suppose that bunch is going to join us, as if there weren't enough of us here already. And oh dear, see how ugly one of those ducklings looks! We're not putting up with him!" Whereupon one of the ducks flew straight over and bit his neck.

"You leave that duckling alone!" said the mother duck. "He's done you no harm."

"Maybe not, but he's big and he looks peculiar," said the duck who had bitten him, "so he deserves a good pecking."

"That mother duck has a handsome family," said the old duck with the red rag around her leg. "All of her children are good-looking except for one, and you must admit he didn't turn out well. She should try hatching him again."

"I'm afraid that's impossible, your ladyship," said the mother duck. "He may not be handsome, but he has a very good nature and he swims beautifully, just as well as the others, maybe even a little better. I think his looks will improve as he grows up, and then he may not seem so big. He spent too long in the egg, that's why he's not quite the right shape." And she gently nipped his neck and smoothed the down on his body. "Anyway, he's a drake," she said, "so it doesn't matter so much. I think he'll be really strong and well able to stand up for himself."

"Well, the other ducklings are very pretty," said the old duck. "Make yourselves at home, my dears, and if you find an eel-head you can bring it to me!"

So they made themselves at home in the poultry yard.

But the poor ugly duckling who had been the last to hatch was pecked and pushed about, and the other ducks and the chickens all made fun of him. "Isn't he big?" they all said, and the turkey cock, who thought himself an emperor because he had been born with spurs, puffed himself up like a ship in full sail, went over to the duckling and gobbled at him, going bright red in the face. The poor duckling didn't know what to do. He was very sad because he looked so ugly and was the laughing-stock of the whole poultry yard.

Well, that was his first day of life, and after it everything went from bad to worse. All the others chased the poor duckling. Even his own brothers and sisters were spiteful to him, and were always saying, "I hope the cat gets you, you ugly thing!" And the mother duck said, "Oh dear, I wish you weren't here!" The ducks bit him, the chickens pecked him, and the girl who fed the poultry put out her foot and kicked him.

So he ran away. He flew over the hedge, and the small birds in the bushes fluttered up into the air in fright. "It's because I'm so ugly," thought the duckling, and he closed his eyes, but he kept on running away all the same. He came to the wide marshes where wild ducks lived, and spent the night there, feeling very tired and very sad.

In the morning the wild ducks flew up, and saw that they had a new companion. "What kind of bird are you?" they asked, and the duckling turned in all directions, saying good morning as politely as he could.

"You're terribly ugly," said the wild ducks, "but that's all the same to us so long as you don't want to marry into our family."

The poor duckling had never thought of marrying at all. He just wanted to be allowed to rest among the reeds and drink a little water in the marshes.

He spent two whole days there, and then two wild geese arrived – or rather wild ganders, for they were males. They hadn't been hatched very long themselves, so they were bold and outspoken.

"Listen, friend," they said. "You're so ugly that we really like you! Would you care to come with us and be a bird of passage? There's another marsh not far from here where some sweet, lovely wild geese live, all of them young ladies who hiss very prettily. An ugly fellow like you could try his luck with them!"

But then there was a loud bang! The sound of shots rang out over the marsh, and both wild geese fell dead in the reeds. Their blood tinged the water red. Bang, bang! The sound came again, great flocks of wild geese rose from the reeds, and more gun-shots were fired.

There was a great hunt going on, and the hunters had surrounded the marsh. Some of them sat perched in the dark trees that rose above the reeds. The blue smoke from their guns hung in the air like mist, drifting over the water. Dogs came splashing through the marshes. The reeds and rushes swayed in all directions. The poor duckling was terrified, and was about to hide his head under his wing when he found himself facing a huge dog. The dog's tongue was hanging out of its mouth and its eyes flashed fiercely. It opened its jaws wide at the sight of the duckling, bared its sharp teeth – and then, with a splash, it was gone again without touching him.

"Oh, thank goodness!" sighed the duckling. "I'm so ugly that even the dog won't bite me!"

So he lay very still while shot after shot echoed above the reeds. It wasn't until late in the day that the firing died down, but still the poor duckling dared not move. He waited some time before looking cautiously around, and then he left the marsh as fast as he could go, chasing over the fields and meadows. The wind was blowing so hard that he had difficulty going forward against it.

In the evening he came to a poor little cottage. It was so tumbledown a place that it hardly knew which side to fall down on, so it stayed standing. The wind was blowing so strongly now that the duckling had to sit down on his tail so as not to be blown away. The storm grew worse and worse, and then he saw that the door of the cottage was hanging off one of its hinges, leaving a gap big enough for him to squeeze through. So he made his way through the gap and into the room.

An old woman lived in the cottage with her hen and her cat, whom she called Sonny. He could arch his back and purr, and his fur gave off sparks if you stroked it the wrong way. The hen had very small, short legs, so she was called Chicky Littlelegs. She laid good eggs, and the old woman loved her like a child.

As soon as morning came the animals saw the strange duckling. The cat began to purr, the hen began to cluck.

"What's the matter?" said the old woman, looking around, but as her eyesight was poor she thought the duckling was a full-grown fat duck which had lost its way. "What a good catch!" she said. "Now I can have duck eggs, unless it's a drake! We'll have to try it and see!"

So the duckling stayed for three weeks to show what he could do, but he didn't lay any eggs. The cat was master of the house, the hen was its mistress, and they were always saying "We and the world," because they really believed they were half the whole world, and the better half too. The duckling thought there could be another opinion about that, but the hen did not agree.

"Can you lay eggs?" she asked.

"No."

"In that case you'd better keep quiet!"

And the cat said, "Can you arch your back and purr, and give off sparks?"

"No."

"Then you ought not to speak up when sensible folk are talking!"

So the duckling sat in a corner feeling cross. He began thinking of the fresh air and the sunlight, and he longed to fly over the water so much that he couldn't help saying so to the hen.

"What on earth is wrong with you?" the hen asked him. "You have nothing to do, that's why you take such peculiar ideas into your head! Lay eggs or purr, and such fancies will all pass over."

"But it's so lovely swimming on the water," said the ducking. "It's wonderful to feel it close over your head, and then to dive down to the bottom."

"That must be a great pleasure, I'm sure!" said the hen. "Really, you're out of your mind! Ask the cat, who is the cleverest creature I know, if he likes swimming on the water or diving down to the bottom. Never mind what I think – ask our mistress the old woman, there's no one cleverer in the world! Do you think she likes swimming and feeling the water close over her head?"

"You don't understand me!" said the duckling.

"Well, if we don't understand you, who will? You surely don't claim to be cleverer than the cat and the old woman, not to mention me? Don't be silly, child. And thank your Creator for all the kindness you've been shown! Haven't you found a warm room here, and companions who can teach you something? Well, you're a fool, and I don't think you at all amusing! Believe me, I mean you well, and I'm telling you these home truths for your own good, which is how you can tell I'm a real friend. So you'd better see about laying eggs, or purring and giving off sparks."

"I think I'm going out into the wide world again," said the duckling.

"You do that!" said the hen.

So the duckling went away. He swam on the water and dived down to the bottom, but he was so ugly that all the other creatures ignored him.

Then summer drew to a close, the leaves in the forest turned yellow and brown, and the wind blew them off the trees. They danced as they fell through the air. The air itself was chilly, and the clouds hung heavy with hail and snow, while a raven sat on a fence croaking with the cold. Just thinking about the weather could make you freeze, and the poor duckling had a hard time.

One evening, when the sun was setting in a beautiful sky, a whole flock of beautiful large birds came out of the bushes. The duckling had never seen anything so lovely. Their plumage was shining white, and they had long, supple necks. They were swans. They uttered a loud cry, spread their magnificent great wings and flew away from that cold place to warmer lands where the lakes were free of ice. They climbed high in the air, very high, and the ugly little duckling was left behind, feeling very strange and sad. He swam around in the water, turning like a millwheel, craned his neck to watch them go, and let out so high and strange a cry that it frightened even himself. Oh, he could never forget those lovely, wonderful birds! Once they were out of his sight he went down to the bottom of the water, and when he came up again he was quite beside himself. He didn't know what birds they were, he didn't know where they were flying, but he loved them as he had never loved anyone before. He didn't envy them, for how could he even wish for such beauty himself? He would have been happy even to be accepted by the ducks, poor ugly creature that he was.

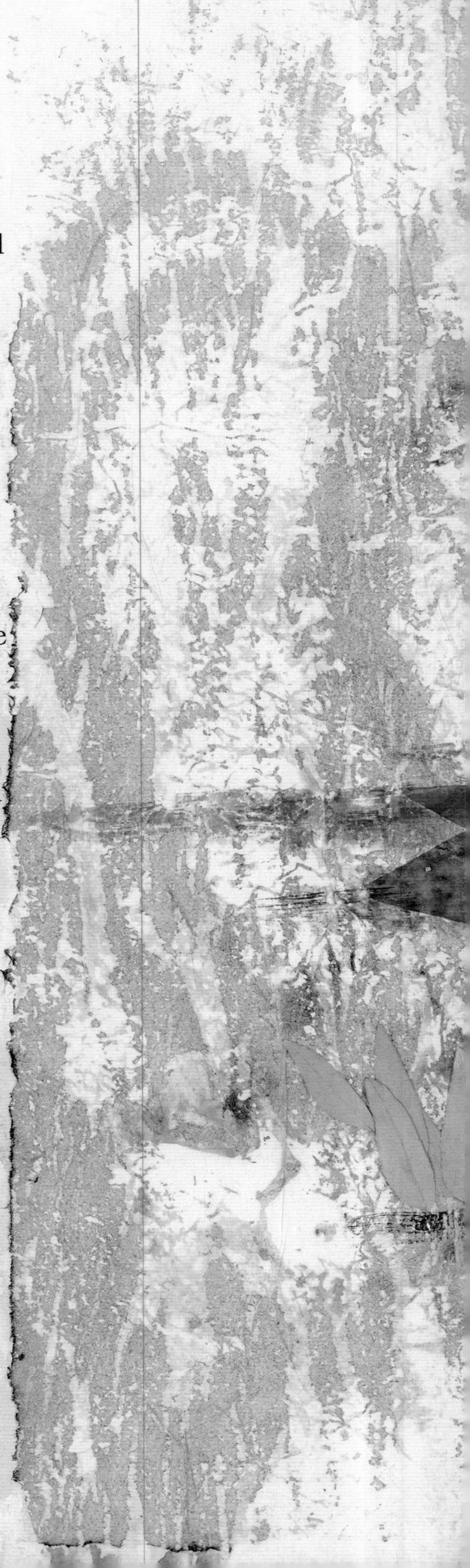

The winter was cold, so cold. The duckling had to keep swimming around in the water to keep it from freezing over, but every night the hole in the ice where he swam grew smaller and smaller. The frost was so hard that the ice creaked. The duckling had to paddle his legs the whole time to keep a space of water open, and in the end he was so weak that he stopped paddling and froze in the ice, stuck fast there.

Early in the morning a farmer came along and saw him. He broke up the ice with his clogs and took the duckling home to his wife, who revived him.

The farmer's children wanted to play with him, but the duckling thought they were going to hurt him, and in his fright he fell into the milk pail, making the milk slop out into the room. The farmer's wife shouted and clapped her hands in the air, and then he flew first into a tub of butter, then into the flour barrel and out again. What a sight he was! The farmer's wife shouted and chased him with the poker, and the children ran about trying to catch the duckling, laughing and screaming. It was a good thing the door was open so that he could escape into the newly fallen snow among the bushes, where he lay as if he were in a trance.

It would be too sad a story to tell you about all the hardship and misery the duckling had to suffer that hard winter. He was sheltering among the reeds in the marsh when the sun began to shine and give some warmth again. Larks were singing – spring, that delightful season, had come.

Then the duckling spread his wings again. They felt stronger than before and bore him powerfully up through the air. Before he knew it he was in a large garden where apple trees and flowers grew, and long green branches bearing fragrant lilac blossom hung above a winding stream. It was all so lovely and green in spring! And then three beautiful swans came out of a thicket of reeds. They ruffled up their feathers and swam gracefully over the water. The duckling recognized the magnificent birds, and was overcome by that strange, sad feeling again.

"I will fly to those royal birds, and they will hack me to death for daring to come near them because I'm so ugly, but I don't mind. I'd rather they killed me than be nipped by the ducks, pecked by the hens, kicked by the girl who looks after the poultry yard, and suffer so much in winter."

So he flew down on the water and swam towards the magnificent swans. They saw him and swam to meet him, ruffling their feathers.

"Kill me!" said the poor bird, and he bent his head and waited for death – but what did he see there in the clear water but his own reflection? He was no longer a clumsy, dingy gray bird, awkward and ugly. He had grown into a swan himself.
Being born in a poultry yard doesn't matter if you hatch out of a swan's egg!

He felt really glad to have been through so much suffering and hardship, because now he could enjoy his own good fortune and the beauty around him all the more. And the big swans swam with him, caressing him gently with their beaks.

Some children came into the garden to throw bread and grain into the water for the birds.

"Oh, look," cried the youngest child, "there's a new one!"

"Yes," cried the other children, "there's a new swan!" And they clapped their hands and danced around, ran to tell their mother and father, and threw bread and cake into the water.

"The new swan is the most beautiful of all!" they said. "So young and so good-looking!" And the older swans bowed to him.

Then he felt quite shy, and hid his head under his wing, hardly knowing what to do. He was wonderfully happy, but he did not feel proud, for a good heart never shows pride. He remembered being despised and persecuted, and now he heard everyone say that he was the loveliest of all the beautiful birds. The lilac bent its green branches down to him as he swam on the water, and the sun shone so warm and bright that he ruffled his feathers, raised his slender neck, and thought joyfully, "I never dreamed of so much happiness when I was the ugly duckling."